THE SECRET LIFE OF PANTS

AND OTHER BRILLIANT NEW POEMS

chosen by

Roger Stevens

Illustrated by Nigel Baines

A & C Black • London

For Lily and Ruby

First published 2006 by
A & C Black Publishers Ltd
38 Soho Square, London, W1D 3HB

www.acblack.com

ISBN 0-7136-7631-0
ISBN 978-0-7136-7631-0

A CIP catalogue for this book is available from the British Library.

This book is produced using paper that is made from wood grown in managed, sustainable forests. It is natural, renewable and recyclable. The logging and manufacturing processes conform to the environmental regulations of the country of origin.

Printed and bound in Great Britain by Bookmarque Ltd, Croydon

Contents

In Praise of Pants

Home Truths

Things You'll Wish Had Been Kept Secret

In Praise of Pants

The Secret Life of Pants

I live with my mates
Screwed up in the drawer
Squashed flat at the back
Passed over. Ignored

Every day in the morning
We're all 'sorted out'
Snatched, grabbed and stared at
And twissled about

Whoever gets lucky
Is pulled on and worn
Which is nice
Because life on a bottom
Is warm!

But it doesn't last long
Till you hear yourself scream
As you're locked in and drowned
In the washing machine

Andrea Shavick

Fig Leaves

Adam's pants were fig leaves
They covered up his bot –
He found them in the bushes
So they didn't cost a lot.

Peter Dixon

The Proud Pants Parade

Silly ones and frilly ones,
Fragrant-as-a-lily ones.

Lacy ones and racy ones,
Extra big and spacey ones.

Spotty ones and dotty ones,
Raggy, baggy, grotty ones.

Cosy ones and rosy ones,
Pretty-as-a-posy ones.

Crummy ones and funny ones,
Cost-a-lot-of-money ones.

Fluffy ones and scruffy ones,
Ancient, velvet, puffy ones.

Plastic ones, fantastic ones,
Superman's elastic ones.

Snowy ones and showy ones,
Flap-about and blowy ones.

Cotton ones and rotten ones,
Better-be-forgotten ones.

Finer ones, designer ones,
Never-seen-diviner ones,

Shiny ones and tiny ones

AND

(just for hedgehogs)

SPINY ONES!

Clare Bevan

Katie Had a Billy Goat

Katie had a billy goat
Which ate Rolos, mints and Snickers
And when she hung the washing out
It gobbled up her knickers!

Angie Turner

This Haiku is Pants

Ants in your pants make
you wriggle and squirm. Giraffes
In your pants are worse

Katharine Crossley

Pants Limerick

A man from Southampton, in Hants,
had a famous collection of pants.
They ranged from the big,
which could smother a pig,
to the small which would barely fit ants.

Trevor Parsons

In the Pink

You'd think a teacher would have more sense
Than to leap over a barbed wire fence
But on a school trip
That's just what ours did
R – I – P!!!
And we saw his *pink* underpants!

Bernard Young

Lucky Pants

Turkey, Germany, Italy, Brazil
Come on lads, let's squash 'em
I've worn these pants for every game
Mum's not allowed to wash 'em

Mum says she'll have to wash 'em soon
They're threatening my health
She was right, I was ill for the very next
  match
So my pants went by themselves

Roger Stevens

Home Truths

There Was a Time

when I couldn't whistle
or ride a bicycle

or use real money
because I hadn't any

or fit puzzle pieces
or tie my own laces

or even begin
to write with a pen

or choose what to eat
or stay up late

or push a wheely basket
at the supermarket

(instead of sitting on it
like a little puppet)

or reach light switches
or strike matches

or climb the stump of a tree
without getting stuck half way

or start the alphabet
and reach the end of it.

Of course I can do
all of those things now

but I couldn't then,
not one of them.

John Mole

My Dad

My dad's bigger than your dad
He's as huge as a grizzly bear
His hands are like cranes
And his head has two brains
And he's totally covered in hair

My dad's smarter than your dad
Though he never tries to impress
He can spell long words
And recite French verbs
And he always wins Scrabble and chess

My dad's tougher than your dad
He has climbed to the top of K2
And he lived on rats
And giant fruit bats
For a year in a cave in Peru

My dad's kinder than your dad
He helps folk who are sad or depressed
And he always finds time
To read us a rhyme
Or give Mum a hug when she's stressed

Roger Stevens

Like You Do

Mum was mad, really mad
We were only playing...
Like you do.

But she was livid, made the walls shake.
We just stood there...
Like you do.

We were only playing though, dressing up
In Mum's best clothes...
Like you do.

How dare you wear my boots!
You'll rip that skirt!
Look at the state of those tights now!
How much lipstick?!

But we were only playing, dressing up
In Mum's new going-out clothes...
Like you do.

It wasn't us, we didn't start it.
Dad was doing it as well, dressing up...
Like you do.

Paul Cookson

Baby Sister

Was I ever that tiny?
Was I wrinkled and skinny?
Did I cry all the time
and pee on your pinny?
Did I sick down my bib
and get covered in poo?

Yes, dear, your sister's
exactly like you.

Roger Stevens

In Church

I lit a candle
And said a prayer
For everyone, everything,
Everywhere.

Then after that
I lit another
And prayed for a rat
Or a baby brother.

Rachel Rooney

My Brother

My brother
goes into his bedroom
puts on his favourite
grunge rock CD,
turns it up really loud,
jumps on his bed
singing louder than the music
and
starts air guitar!
He waves his right arm
up and down
like a crazy windmill
banging the strings
his fingers twitch and move
at a hundred miles per hour

as his face contorts
in weird air guitar poses.

Then he jumps off his bed
and lands on his knees,
sliding along the shiny timber floor
still playing
furious air guitar.
Mum smiles.
Dad shakes his head.
I'm trying to do homework
so I ask Mum
if he could turn it down,
and what does she say:
'In a minute. Let him have his fun.'

My brother is 26 years old.

Steven Herrick

Sorting Out the Falling Out

Ryan used to be my friend
but now he drives me round the bend
It's all broken, it won't mend
I hate him.

It happened yesterday in Games
he tripped me up, I called him names
it was his fault, it's me he blames
he hates me.

We've known each other since Year Three
me for him and him for me
that's in the past because you see
I hate him.

This morning I did try to smile
he pulled a face and ran a mile
reckons he's best mates with Kyle
I'll kill him.

At break time he came up to say
sorry, but I walked away
I've got other games to play
so ner-ner.

Deep inside I'm really sad
and I expect that he feels bad
my best friend, a dead good lad
I hate it

We should try to clear the air
he's only sitting over there
come on Ryan, let's be fair.
It's crazy!

Good, he's walking over here
with a smile from ear to ear
you should hear the class all cheer
All right then!

We shake hands, the anger's out
it makes us jump and laugh and shout
the best of friends again, no doubt.
It's sorted.

David Harmer

Postcard From the Garden Shed

Dear All,
I sit inside the garden shed
I have lots of food, so I'm well fed,
I have a kettle to make my tea
And a blanket to put over me.
I have a chair so I can rest
And a friendly spider – a hairy pest.
I can play my music as loud as I like,
I can fiddle around with my bike.
I can make a mess and not clear it away
And I can't hear the arguing when you play.
I love you all, I know you love me,
But my shed provides some therapy!
Love Dad X

Coral Rumble

Mum's Grave

It's in a quiet and peaceful spot, I guess
It's made of marble
There are trees, dead leaves and grass

And by the headstone is a wooden letter box
Where we can post our memories
I don't use it a lot
I mainly say a prayer
And let it rise into the cloudy sky
Above Mum's grave
Because she's not down there

Mum's grave is just a line
That's written underneath the word goodbye

Roger Stevens

Grandad's Woollen Scarf

It was Grandad's funeral today.
I wore his red, woollen scarf.

Grandma said it would keep me warm
And remind me of happier times.
It did.
It had his smell
And the thought of him
Kept me warm
All day.

Grandad's woollen scarf.

Lisa Watkinson

Things You'll Wish Had Been Kept Secret

Bad Habits

Don't pick your nose
It isn't polite
And God didn't give us
nails to bite.

Don't scratch your bum
Don't slurp your tea.
I want you to grow up
and be like me.

Sometimes Mum
makes me mad.
Why can't I grow up
and be like Dad?

Roger Stevens

Well-kept Secret

He lives inside my bedroom
My very special pet
I've had my skunk for five years now
and no one's noticed yet.

Paul Cookson

Don't Snog Frogs
(a confession and a warning)

Don't snog frogs –
the prospect of finding
just one in a million
who was once a prince
is slim indeed.

Don't snog frogs –
there's a bigger chance
of a lottery win
than finding the boy of your dreams
in a stream.

Consider snogging
the messiest boy in your school
the one who leaves great traces
of lunch, smeared round his face –
well it's worse than that!

I once thought the quick route
to a wonderful life could be mine,
if I only took the time to find
the right amphibian.

I searched and searched
from night till day

trying to find that Mr Right,
listening out for that deep bass croak,
an indication that my prince
had spoken.

I must have snogged a million frogs,
finding them in lakes or under logs,
feeling their rough and leathery skin
touch my lips.

So don't snog frogs.
Your life is not a fairy tale
you are not a princess
in waiting.

Hop off, hop away,
don't pause, don't stay,
don't ever imagine
your dreams will come true.
I tell you, frog snogging
just isn't for you.

Briony Moses

Mary Didn't Have a Little Lamb

No!

Mary had a little slug
its skin was tough and green
and when the slug refused to budge
oh gosh, was there a scene!

You should have heard our Mary yell
'I need you slug – for Show & Tell!
It's time for school – now come on, please!'
She even got down on her knees

But slug was not one to be swayed
and poor old Mary was dismayed
when slug set off and waltzed to school –
all four miles – the crazy fool!

So how to end this oddly tale?
Did slug succeed, give up or fail?
Well, slug did make it to the gate
(of the school) some two years late!

One half term – so had to wait
till Monday morning – by the gate
But having come so very far
was flattened by a teacher's car

James Carter

Puppy Dog

I wish I was a puppy dog,
Life would be such fun,
I'd frisk around without my clothes,
Then sit and lick my...

ears and nose.

Jane Clarke

The Early Bird's Breakfast

Worm steak
Worm soufflé
Worm cake
Worm flambé
Worm custard
Worm strudels
Worm mustard
Worm noodles
Worm parts
Worms – shredded
Worm tarts
Worms – breaded
Worm's cream
Worms braised
Worm Supreme
Worms glazed
Worms diced
Worms puffed
Worms iced
Worms – stuffed

Birds will say
In clearest terms
They just can't get
Enough of worms

Robert Scotellaro

Painful Bliss

Have you ever
Have you ever
Had a pimple on your bottom?
And you squeeze it
Yes, you squeeze it
Coz it's hurting something rotten?

And your eyes run
Yes, your eyes run
As you squeeze it good and proper,
But you're happy
Yes, you're happy
Coz it really was a whopper.

Clive Webster

Spring Cleaning

I'm cleaning out my bedroom
and finding loads of things:
three twenty ps,
a DVD,
the last book of
Lord of the Rings,
two floppy disks,
blue sunglasses,
my pen-pal's lost address...

Such fun, sorting out a mess:
best of all,
a slice of pizza;
crusty,
fuzzy,
fluffy.
Who knows how old?

Just pop it in the microwave –
mmm, maybe I'll eat it
cold.

Mike Johnson

Toe Sucking

Mum said,
Sucking your toe
Is a horrid habit

Stop it at once!

And Grandad,
Put your socks back on!

Roger Stevens

Poems With Secrets

Flower

I am a tumbler
A current
A splasher
A flower

I'm always rushing
When I'm young
But when I'm old
I am slower

Roger Stevens

(a stream)

A Thoughtful Riddle

At first a forest,
Followed by a field,
Hedged by two swords
And underneath, two spheres
And after two threads
And at last the nightingale singing

Albanian riddle ***(translated by Elona Velca and Andrew Fusek Peters)***

(a face)

Wise Words

Here comes a creature
on two heavy feet.

Staring with his one eye
up and down the street.

He listens with two ears,
shakes two hundred heads.

Has only one mouth
from which wise words are said.

Who speaks them?

Joan Poulson

(an intelligent garlic-seller with a telescope)

What Am I?
(here's a fistful of clues)

Help lender
Mail sender
Warm greeter
Card cheater
Yawn hider
Pen guider
Gift taker
Sign maker
Door knocker
Jaw socker
Tight gripper
Ear clipper
Five scorer
Explorer!

Philip Waddell

(a hand)

There Stands an Oak

There stands an oak
And from that oak,
twelve branches grow,
And on each branch,
nests two plus two
And in each nest,
seven eggs bright blue

Czech riddle ***(translated by Andrew Fusek Peters)***

(year / months / weeks / days)

Warning

I am alive and a friend to all
I wear many coats –
some large, some small.

Sometimes I'm red,
sometimes brown,
sometimes white.

If you chop off my head
beware of my bite.

What am I?

Joan Poulson

(An onion)

New School Riddle

I am the cold shiver and your churning
  stomach
The wall of new faces that don't talk to you
The sound of a snigger as you pass
The party invites quickly hidden
The taste of school dinners you don't want
  to eat
Needle sharp
A spot full of pus
I'm bigger than you and there are more of us.
I am the tremble in your voice
You don't fit in
Echoes round your head
Too tall, too thin, too small, too fat
You'll never make friends
You're no good at anything
Least of all that

Oh yes, in my grip
I'll hold you back.

Katharine Crossley

(fear)

As I Was Going to St Fred's!

As I was going to St Fred's
I saw a man with seven heads
And on each head were seven ears
And from both eyes dropped seven tears!
Tears, ears, eyes and heads –

How many minutes are there in an hour?

Ian Bland

Heart

If you stood upon the moon
What would you see?
Rearrange my heart
It's what you mean to me

Roger Stevens

(the Earth)

You Can't Scare Me!

Nothing Frightens Me

I'm afraid of nothing
Nothing frightens me
So when I see nothing coming
I pack my bags...

And flee!

Bernard Young

You Can't Scare Me, Whoever You Are

This house ISN'T haunted –
It's only a tale!
So don't try to scare me
You're certain to fail!
There's really NO POINT
In you making that *din*,
I'm locking the door
And I *won't* let you in!
I think that you're clinking
A *bicycle* chain –
You're howling TOO LOUD
And you laugh like a drain.
I can *guess* how you're making
Those THUMPS on the stairs –
I expect you are bouncing a ball.

And now you are there
At the foot of my bed;
Tell me...

How did you float through the wall?

Trevor Harvey

Marie Celeste

It's hard now to remember straight
but there was something in the air –
it was eerie, desolate.

We sighted her at just past eight
but who first noticed her decks were bare?
It's hard now to remember. Straight

away we called the crew, the mate,
the steersman – no one anywhere –
it was eerie, desolate.

We saw the rigging in a state,
flapping about with no one there.
It's hard now to remember straight

what happened next. At any rate,
for those of us who boarded her
it was eerie – desolate:

warm food, a half-empty plate,
a recently vacated chair.
It's hard now to remember straight

we were so scared. As for their fate –
had they got sick, gone mad? I swear
though, in that eerie, desolate

ship, it was chilling to speculate.
We felt glad to get out of there.
It's hard now to remember straight –
but it was eerie, desolate.

Jill Townsend

The Greedy Ghost

In the seaside town of Scarborough
On the North Yorkshire coast,
There stands a grand hotel of which
The local people boast
That it's, for years, been haunted by
The world's most greedy ghost.

In the kitchen after midnight
You can smell its ghostly toast,
And on Sundays after sunset
Yorkshire pud and ghostly roast,
And many folks who've stayed there claim
They've seen their ghostly host.

And, according to a story
Published in the *Yorkshire Post*,
Everybody sees it chewing
As if totally engrossed.
And nightly in the neighbourhood
I'm told you are supposed
To hear loud ghostly belching and
One night I did... almost!

Nick Toczek

Riddle Me a Count

My first is in blood and twice in undead.
My second is in nightmare and also in dread.
My third is in fangs but not in doom.
My fourth is in coffin but not in tomb.
My fifth's in bloodsucker but not in vein.
My sixth's in bloodcurdling, and not in
  bloodstain.
My last is in vampire but not in bite.
  I rise from my grave on the stroke of
midnight!

John Foster

(Dracula)

Fragment of a Poem Found by a Lake

The lake is as calm
As an upturned sky

We sit amidst daisies and buttercups
In dappled willow shade

You are reading a comic
I am writing a poem

A silence startles us
Birds freeze in mid flight

The lake shimmers,
Ripples, churns

A dark shape rises like an upset paint pot
Black on blue sugar paper

It blots out the sun
The sky is full of hissing

Panic!

Run...

Roger Stevens

A Presence

Banging noises,
clanking chain.
Could be the toilet
gone wrong again.
The sound of footsteps
on the floor.
A cold draught.
Shut the door.
Something
creepy
in the
house
and I
can't
sleep.

I'm only a mouse.

Jill Townsend

The Door

Do not open the door!
Maybe inside there is
a seething cauldron,
a wild-tailed dragon,
or a teacher's eye, staring...

Do not open the door!
Maybe a snake slithers,
four walls
like an invisible clock
tick away
a never-ending morning.
A teacher's tongue
wags in the darkness
with *your* name on its tip...

Do not open the door!
Maybe the ghost of Voldemort
lurks in the shadows,
waiting...

Do not open the door!
Maybe
through the breathing darkness
a gnarled, insistent finger
silently unfurls to point
to someone...

It
has chosen

YOU!

Judith Nicholls
(*with apologies to Miroslav Holub!*)

Grand Master Myster-ie

If you're about at midnight
Tune in to Myster-ie
He's rappin' king of the underworld
A free-styling zombie

He's the meanest monster DJ
Who plays the top ten tombs
A hit at every party
With vampires, spooks and ghouls

He's always where it's happening
Performing with 'The Chilly Bones'
Jammin' it with Spook Dog
'Hex Club Five' and the 'Re-Moans'

A real smooth operator
Ghosting radio and TV
If you want your coffin rocking
It's 'Spook Real Time', RIP

So get chilling with the 'Shivers'
Or if you like to 'Rattle and Roll'
Tune into 'Spook Real Time'
The station for lost souls.

Sue Hardy-Dawson

Sssh...
Don't Tell Anyone But These Poems Are BONKERS!

If Houses Went on Holiday

Wouldn't it be great
if when you went on holiday
your house could go on holiday, too?
Whole terraces could disappear together
for boozy weekends in Ibiza.
Semi-detacheds could rekindle romance
side by side on moonlit beaches.
You'd find bungalows backpacking
and chalets criss-crossing the Channel.
Detached houses going solo
seeking dates or mates on singles trips,
while apartment blocks could take package
  tours

jetting to Jamaica in jumbos.
Just imagine houses hitting the holiday trail,
forming orderly queues on major roads
then crowding holiday beaches.
Imagine houses surfing or sunbathing,
jumping into swimming pools, keeping cool.
See them paragliding or rock climbing,
scuba diving or horse riding.
So much better than brooding, silent and
  empty,
rooms filled with gloom, windows
like sad eyes, blinking back tears.
How much better it would be for houses
to have a holiday break like us!

Brian Moses

Oh, You Shouldn't Have!

I brought you a cauliflower
I thought that a rose
Was too much the same sort of red as
your nose.

I brought you an oak tree
I thought that a cake
Was a little too much for your waistline
to take.

I brought you a haddock
I thought you'd prefer
A fish to a flower – to show that I care.

I would have brought perfumed silk sheets
for your bed
But I didn't, so here is a bullfrog instead.

Jan Dean

Our Dog's Birthday

Our dog's birthday
is February 31st, he said.

But there isn't
a February 31st, I said.

That's right, he said,
And we haven't got dog.

John Foster

My Not Favourite Things

Doorknobs and chickens
And mouldy green chocolates
Shoe trees and dead bees
And ice cream in pockets
Spent tunes and bent spoons
Bananas with wings
These are a few of my not favourite things

Stories about Ron
Who hides in the evenings
TV with nought on
And Spiderman key rings
Gristle and thistles
And some songs of Sting's
These are a few of my less favourite things

When the pear drops
When a fool stops
When I grow a beard
I simply re-varnish my old bits of string
And then I don't feeeeeeeeeeeeeeeeeeeeeeel
Soooooooooooooo
Weird

Roger Stevens

The Bicycle's Birthday

Scoff and sneer all you like
I'm having a birthday for my bike
Why are you laughing? What did I say?
Oh silly me! I got it round the wrong way.

Alison Hunt

The Lost Poem

Justin Coe

Change of Position

I had been standing on my teacher's two feet
For some time
When she remarked –
Stand on your own two feet
For once!

Roger Stevens

A Week of Difficulties Involving Cucumbers

Monday – I went to the bakers
To buy some bread and pies
But the French stick turned out
To be
A cucumber in disguise.

Tuesday – I was having a bath
So imagine my surprise
When I grabbed the bar of soap
And found
A cucumber in disguise.

Wednesday – I went out walking until
Rain fell from the skies
But when I took out my umbrella
It was
A cucumber in disguise.

Thursday – Played St George in drama
The Queen said, 'Sir Knight, Arise!'
And gave to me a magic sword
That was
A cucumber in disguise.

Friday – I was racing in the relay
We were going to take first prize
But the baton I held turned out
To be
A cucumber in disguise.

Saturday – was my brother's birthday
And tears poured from his eyes
As my present of a baseball bat
Was just
A cucumber in disguise.

Sunday – Granny stayed for lunch
But as we wished her fond goodbyes
I found that I was waving
Yes, yes
A cucumber in disguise.

John Coldwell

Writer's Block

2B or not 2B
That is the pencil.

Lucinda Jacob

And Now... If We Could Be Serious For a Moment

A Kingfisher Day

I leaned on the bridge
Feeling dull and downhearted
When out of the willows
A kingfisher darted.
In a blue streak it flashed
Down the river away.
Lifted my spirits,
Rescued my day.

Eric Finney

Famous Friends

I'm mates with Michael Owen
And I come from Liverpool
I watch each match from the dugout
It's really cool

I'm Johnny Depp's mate
I've been in films a lot
You see me in the crowd scenes
And sometimes I get shot

I'm a friend of Kylie
The singing star, you know
I once sang on her CD
She said I stole the show

I've got so many famous friends
It leads to jealousy
That's why I'm on my own today
So... stay and play with me

Please...

Roger Stevens

Tornado

I knew a girl: a tornado,
born on a storm.
Arrived in a whirl, with a thump
on the hospital floor.

Picked herself up, found her feet
but still she was reeling.
The world was a blur; off-kilter.
And all she kept feeling

was dizzy and queasy and dazed.
To stop herself churning
she did what she needed to do,
and carried on turning

Like a coin, a top, a wheel,
the floss on a stick
or the drum of a washing machine
as it reaches its peak,

she span faster. Her arms outstretched
like blades of a chopper.
She rose from this world into space.
Nothing on earth could stop her.

Rachel Rooney

The Sofa and the Rocking Chair

The sofa sighed to the rocking chair:
'I wish I could be more like you
And tap in time to the beat of a rhyme
and send off to sleep the person who
Sits in my arms like you do.'

The rocking chair said to the sofa:
'How I wish I could do what you do –
To not be so rootless and restless
And seat not one person, but two –
I'd happily give up my rocking
If I could be steadfast like you!'

Colin West

Half Rhymes

Like the picture you show Miss Card
who says, That isn't too bad

Or the scarf you give to Aunt Flower
who says, That isn't my colour

Or when your best friend is playing catch
and she says, If you like, you can watch

Or the day that you thought wouldn't come
and you walk to school on your own

Roger Stevens

Blessings

The bout of flu,
The broken bone,
The out-of-order telephone;
The missed coach trip,
The delayed plane,
The punctured tyre,
The cancelled train.

The aisle and not the window seat,
The kid you didn't want to meet;
The failed exam,
The second prize...
Sometimes they're hard to recognise.

Philip Waddell

A Snail Tries to Understand Prejudice

Does my skin bother you?
Elephants are grey.
You love elephants. Is it because
Elephants have floppy ears and swinging
  trunks?
Which one of you would stomp on an
  elephant?

Is my casing a problem?
Turtles have shells.
You love turtles.
Is it because
Turtles have cute flippers and old man's faces?
Which one of you would drown a turtle in
  stale beer?

Is my single foot an issue?
Flamingos stand on one foot.
You love flamingos.
Is it because flamingos have curved beaks
  and pretty pink feathers?
Which one of you would poison a flamingo?

Is it my speed you object to?
Sloths are slow.
You love sloths.

Is it because
Sloths have funny faces and hang upside
  down?
Which one of you would throw a sloth over
  next-door's fence?

Or do you hate me
Because
I share your love
Of lettuce?

John Coldwell

Best Friend

Didn't know that day we met
Six years old on the seesaw
At the park
That we'd become best friends for ever.

I liked football – was good at it
He didn't – two left feet
So we played soldiers instead.

I took him to my house
Who've you brought home this time?
moaned Dad, distracted,
Painting a wall from high up a ladder.

We drank milky coffee
and watched Dad painting

Then my dog came over and bit him.

Ian Bland

You Can't Keep a Laugh a Secret For Long

Laughing

I was laughing fit to bust
Laughing so much
I thought I'd pop
All the buttons on my shirt
I laughed so much
It hurt

I just couldn't stop laughing
What a hoot!
I thought my sides would split
They did!
And what's more
All my funny bones
Fell out on the floor!

Michael Leigh

It's Easy to Laugh

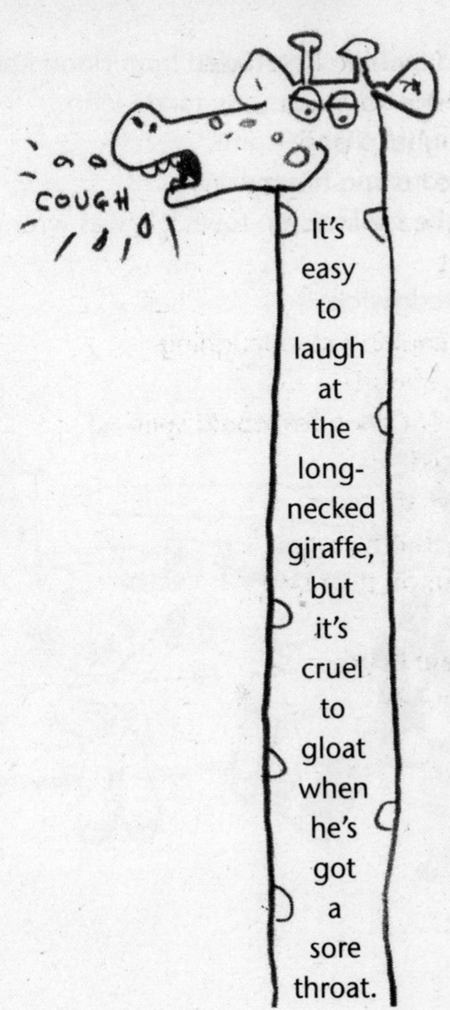

It's
easy
to
laugh
at
the
long-
necked
giraffe,
but
it's
cruel
to
gloat
when
he's
got
a
sore
throat.

Poet Unknown

Nose

A head teacher who hailed from Hong Kong
Had a nose that was one-metre long.
He thought that the girls
Were admiring his curls
When he walked into town. He was wrong.

Fred Sedgwick

Boulderdash!

A pebble
Is no rebel
Till it gets a
Little older...

When fully grown
Into a stone
It's then a
Little boulder

Graham Denton

Sick Note

The teacher needs a letter
now I'm back at school and better
Not that I've been ill.
I spent the day in Rhyl.

Lisa Watkinson

Mirror Image

I practised
With my guitar
Before the mirror
In my room
Holding the guitar
By the neck
And swinging
Cunning ground strokes
Dazzling serves
Lazy lobs
And thunderous volleys

One day I'll be
The world's greatest
Tennis player

Roger Stevens

Cheering Mum Up

I picked a flower for my mum
when she was sad and looking glum.
She smiled as she took the rose
and sniffed some greenfly up her nose.

Jill Townsend

Sebastian Angus McFee

Sebastian Angus McFee
Was born and brought up in a tree.
He loved little birds,
But said some rude words,
When one went and pooed in his tea.

Pat Gadsby

Fighting Sleep

Bed!
they said.
I'll never sleep!
I whined...

But then,
somehow, I find
sleep creeps
into my mind.

For goodness' sake,
I'm wide awake!
I lie.
Sleep stares me in the eye.

I try
to raise my head,
to slide down from my bed.
My back is lead.

N – O – W!
sleep sighs
and gently closes
both my eyes.

Judith Nicholls